This book belongs to:

_____

Other books about Melric the Magician:

Melric and the Sorcerer
Melric the Magician who Lost His Magic
Melric and the Petnapping
Melric and the Dragon

This paperback edition first published in 2017 by Andersen Press Ltd.
First published in Great Britain in 2016 by Andersen Press Ltd.,
20 Vauxhall Bridge Road, London SW1V 2SA.
Copyright © David McKee, 2016.
The rights of David McKee to be identified as the author and illustrator
of this work have been asserted by him in accordance with the
Copyright, Designs and Patents Act, 1988.
All rights reserved.
Colour separated in Switzerland by Photolitho AG, Zürich.
Printed and bound in Malaysia.

1  3  5  7  9  10  8  6  4  2

British Library Cataloguing in Publication Data available.
ISBN 978 1 78344 538 7

# Melric

## AND THE CROWN

# David McKee

ANDERSEN PRESS

Melric the magician was going to visit Kra the wise man.
"Don't forget the ceremony of the crown," said the King as Melric left.
Every year the King proved his right to rule by walking under an
enchanted waterfall. If the crown was genuine, and of course it always
was, a rainbow appeared and the crowd chanted, "Long live the King!"
That was the ceremony of the crown.

After Melric had gone, the King played with his pet Troon
and watched the soldiers parade with their dragon mascot.

That evening the crown was missing.
"It had better be here in the morning," said the King.

The next morning, the servants came to say they still couldn't find the crown. But to their surprise the King was wearing it. "It was here when I woke up," the King explained. "It must have been the Troon playing tricks."

Meanwhile, Kra was teaching Melric, his sister Mertel and cousin Guz
a spell using water to show them whatever they wished to see.
"Show me the King's crown," said Melric, thinking of the ceremony.
The pool became a screen and there was the crown. "But that's Sondrak
wearing it," said Melric, recognising his old enemy. "Where is the King?"

The picture changed. There was the King, also with a crown.
Kra explained. "You asked to see the crown. Sondrak has it. The gnome goldsmiths made a copy that he swapped for the real crown."
"But the King will fail the test," said Melric. "Sondrak will be king. I must go."

As Melric set off for the castle Kra said, "Remember, Melric, what's been done once can be done again."

Melric arrived at the castle while the King was in his bath.
He left again at once, with the fake crown.

"Oh no, not again," said the King when he saw the crown was missing.
"Now where have you put it?" he asked the Troon.

While the King searched, Melric went to the house of the gnome goldsmiths. He hid as they returned home for the night.

When all was quiet, Melric used a water barrel and Kra's spell to see Sondrak. He was inside the house, wearing the crown and ordering gnomes to get firewood.

The firewood was near Melric. Quickly he put a spell on the wood and then hid as the gnomes came to collect it.

As the wood burned the spell began to work. The fire gave off a pleasant smell that sent Sondrak and the gnomes into a deep sleep. Melric let himself into the house and exchanged the crowns. Then he returned to the castle to replace the real crown.

In the morning the King was making a terrible commotion.
"What's all this fuss about?" asked Melric.
"Thank goodness you're back," said the King. "The Troon
is playing silly tricks with the crown. You'd better look after
him until after the ceremony."

The ceremony started as usual. The King led a procession to the waterfall where the people waited, but as he approached, a shout came from the other side.

"Behold the crown!" cried Sondrak. The crowd gasped and he continued:

"I am your King,
to me you'll bow down,
when you see the proof
by test of the crown."

Sondrak stepped under the waterfall and
waited for the rainbow: it never came. Instead
the water poured directly on him, sending
him into the lake below. The crowd chanted,
"Imposter!" and laughed and laughed.
Sondrak couldn't stand being laughed at.

Melric explained everything to the King who said, "If it weren't for you, Melric, that would be me in the water." Then he called out:

"I am your King
and I'll do my best
to serve if my crown
passes the test."

He stood under the waterfall and the rainbow appeared.
"Long live the King!" roared the crowd.
Melric watched Sondrak leave. "I wonder what
he'll try next time?" he thought.